Sleeping Beauty

ILLUSTRATED BY
KINUKO Y. CRAFT

AS RETOLD BY
MAHLON F. CRAFT

SeaStar Books

New York

Text © 2002 by Mahlon F. Craft
Illustrations © 2002 by Kinuko Y. Craft

SeaStar Books
A division of North-South Books Inc.

First published in the United States in 2002 by
SeaStar Books,
a division of North-South Books Inc., New York.
Published simultaneously in Great Britain, Canada,
Australia, and New Zealand by North-South Books,
an imprint of Nord-Süd Verlag AG, Gossau Zürich,
Switzerland.

The artwork for this book was
prepared by using oil over watercolor on
Strathmore™ illustration board.

The text for this book is set in
Adobe Koch Antiqua.

Book design by Mahlon F. Craft

Library of Congress Cataloging-in-Publication Data
is available.

A CIP catalogue record for this book is available from
The British Library.

ISBN 1-58717-120-1 (trade edition)
1 3 5 7 9 HC 10 8 6 4 2
ISBN 1-58717-121-X (library edition)
1 3 5 7 9 LE 10 8 6 4 2

Printed in Hong Kong

For more information about our books, and the authors and artists who create them, visit our web site:
www.northsouth.com

For hope

 nce upon a time there lived a King and Queen whose fondest desire was to have a child—"A little one to bounce on our knee," as they wistfully said every day. A year passed, then three, yet they remained without child still.

Just when the loving couple thought their wish would remain forever unfulfilled, the Queen began to bathe at a secluded pool where there lived an ancient frog. She sang to the old creature as sweetly as she would to a child of her own. To the Queen's great surprise, one day the frog sprang from his perch and began to speak. "To one far more fair than I should song so sweet be sung. Within twelve months' time a daughter to you shall be born."

And just as the frog said, a little girl was soon born to the Queen. The King was so overcome with joy that he could barely contain himself. The child was called Aurora, and the King ordered a great christening feast to celebrate. Every relative, friend, and any other acquaintance of importance was invited, and the royal squires were sent to search out all of the fairies who inhabited his realm.

ow it happened that to invite the fairies required very special golden place settings for each. The King had just twelve and they were very costly indeed— even for a king. When the squires returned and announced that thirteen fairies were living in his lands, the King became quite vexed, for his treasuries were nearly as dear to him as his daughter. But when he learned the thirteenth was a very old fairy who had not been seen for more than fifty years, the King happily concluded, "She must be either dead or under some spell. Surely there is no need to inquire further."

When at last the ceremonies were over, the guests retired to the King's palace where the attendance of the fairies was to be celebrated at the feast. Each of the twelve places was set in magnificent style indeed, with plates and cups of beaten gold and a jewelled chest containing a knife, fork, and spoon, all inlaid with precious stones. The table was laid with bowls and glasses of crystal and all was set aglitter by candles too numerous to count.

After a splendid meal each fairy presented the child with a magic gift. One gave virtue, another wisdom, a third beauty, and so on, until the Princess Aurora had been assured nearly every good fortune in life. Just as the eleventh fairy bestowed her wish, the thirteenth fairy—who was very much alive after all—appeared in a flash.

nd now you may have MY gift!" the old fairy exclaimed angrily. "On her sixteenth birthday, the Princess shall prick herself with a spindle and die!" Without another word, she turned and stormed out of the hall.

The fearful prophecy caused the guests to shudder, and the gentler souls among them wept. Almost out of their wits with grief, the King and Queen now despaired of the terrible cost of the King's rash and selfish decision to ignore the thirteenth fairy.

But now the twelfth fairy, whose gift was still unspoken, stepped forward. "Your Majesties! Calm yourselves. Although my powers cannot alter my elder sister's terrible wish, the Princess shall not die. Instead Aurora shall fall into a deep sleep that will last one hundred years."

With that, she and all of the rest of the fairies vanished.

he very next morning the King's squires carried decrees to the farthest corners of his land commanding every spindle be immediately destroyed. By this the King sought to protect his child from the misfortune he had caused, and as years passed so it seemed he had. Meanwhile, the other fairies' gifts were all fulfilled, and Aurora grew into a maiden of great beauty, so gentle, kind, and clever that everyone who happened upon her could not help but love her.

On the day of her sixteenth birthday, the King and Queen had gone out to find a very special gift and the Princess was left in the castle, free to do as she pleased. She looked about in every curious place, exploring as she might choose.

Finally, she came to the entrance to an old tower. At the top of the tower's winding staircase, she came upon a door which suddenly sprang open all of its own accord. There sat an old woman, spinning flax.

"Good day, good woman," Aurora said politely. "What are you doing here?"

"Dear child, I am spinning," said the old woman. "Do you find it interesting?"

"Oh yes! It looks such a merry thing to do," the Princess said. "May I try too?"

"Why of course, my dear," the old woman said. "But mind the spindle," she added cunningly, "for it has very special powers."

Indeed, the moment the wheel began to turn, the spindle threw off a shower of glowing lights in every direction. "How beautiful!" Aurora exclaimed. Enchanted, she could not resist examining the spinning shaft. But the instant she touched it, the sharp point pricked her finger.

The old fairy—for that is who the old woman really was—smiled, revelling in her deed, then vanished without a trace. The Princess collapsed on the floor and the spell immediately took hold.

 t once, sleep fell over the entire palace and an eerie silence came over all. In the stables the horses knelt and slept, the doves in the eaves stopped cooing, and even the dragonflies upon the moat ceased to stir. The fire upon the hearth died away, and the cook, who had just caught his lazy kitchen-lad by the scruff of the neck, lost his hold and they tumbled apart like two court jesters, snoring loudly. The wind stopped and not even the tiniest spiderweb stirred so much as the breadth of a hair.

When the King and Queen returned and beheld the cruel work of the old fairy, their eyes welled up with tears and they sobbed uncontrollably. All their efforts had been in vain.

Deep in sorrow, the King and Queen lovingly laid their daughter on a bed covered with the finest embroidery in the most elegant room atop the tallest tower. Aurora's soft cheeks were flushed delicately as the petals of a rose, and though her eyes were indeed closed, the gentle rise and fall of her bosom made it plain she was still alive.

hen this happened, the twelfth fairy—whose wish had saved Aurora from the eternal sleep—was far away, leagues beyond a distance that could be travelled by mortal souls. She knew instantly of the misfortune and speedily arrived in a chariot of fire drawn by dragons. When the King beheld this sight he drew back in fear, such was his guilt over his daughter's plight. Nevertheless he went down to the gates of his palace and with a mournful face, offered his hand to welcome her.

nce again, the Majesties were comforted by the good fairy. Then, as she bid them good-bye, she touched the grieving couple with her wand, and they—like all the rest—fell fast asleep. Briars suddenly sprang up out of the earth and grew around the castle. Every moment the bramble, full of thorny spikes, grew taller and wider until only the very tip of the tower where Aurora lay remained visible to give any clue of what lay within.

From the mysterious thorny tangle there soon spread throughout the land the legend of Briar Rose, as the sleeping Princess became known. From time to time, princes heard of the legend and set out on vain quests to penetrate the hedge and reach the castle. Though many a gallant young prince entered, even when fully clad in battle dress, none was ever seen again.

fter many years, when no one any longer bothered to challenge the fearful briars, a young Prince from a faraway land found his way into the kingdom. The tenderhearted lad kept a falcon as a companion. When he loosed it for exercise it flew immediately high above the bramble where it circled curiously 'round and 'round. The moment the Prince's eyes fell upon the tower he had to know what lay inside.

Now the curious Prince asked everyone he came upon about the tower in the bramble. Some said it was infested with evil spirits; others said it was used by sorcerers. And many believed there lived a powerful ogre who carried off wayward children to eat for tasty morsels after dinner.

Finally one day the Prince came upon an old peasant woman, hobbled by age. She told of the Legend of the Briars—how behind them stood the tower of a great castle where slept a princess beautiful beyond words called Briar Rose. She told of how the Princess had lain in slumber nearly a hundred years together with the King and Queen and all their court. But she also told the young Prince of the many others who had come to the mysterious briars only to disappear into them, never again to find their way back.

The handsome youth would not be daunted. "No matter what the outcome, I must make my way to the tower!" he declared. The thought of a sleeping beauty such as Briar Rose lying unprotected in a thorny prison was more than his good and valiant nature could bear.

he Prince prepared as though for a great battle, yet when he set upon the first thorny branch, to his amazement it only fell away harmlessly before him. A wide opening appeared. As he strode into it, the bramble immediately closed behind so that his retinue was barred from following. Still the Prince continued without the slightest fear.

He soon arrived at a large forecourt. Around him everywhere lay the bodies of men, women, and animals. A fearful silence and the semblance of death lay over all. But then the Prince realized a ruddy blush never found on the dead lay over the porters' faces. Their plates, still laden with half-eaten food, revealed that sleep had taken them even as they dined. As he went on, he found courtier and servant alike fast asleep, and in the hall above the King and Queen rested just as they had collapsed. Everything was just as the old peasant had told.

The silence was so great, the Prince could hear the beating of his own heart as he came to the tower where Briar Rose slept. When at last he reached the door to her chamber, it swung away of its own accord, and there was revealed the sleeping Princess. As if beholding a slumbering angel, the Prince could not turn away his gaze. The power of her beauty was such that he immediately bent over and kissed her delicate lips.

A clock struck the hour. One hundred years after she pricked her finger, the Princess opened her eyes. Her enchantment was broken.

ow long have I waited for this moment, my Prince!" exclaimed the Princess with a tender glance, and they immediately fell in love and embraced.

Barely able to form words to express his happiness, the Prince said "Can it truly be that the eyes of this angel I now behold open only for me?"

"Yes, sweet Prince!" Aurora replied. "These many long years only you have filled my dreams, for none other could awaken me from my spell. Now in love's sweet name at last our hearts will together be eternally bound."

Arm-in-arm, Prince and Princess went first to the King and Queen whom they immediately awakened. When they beheld their daughter and her adoring escort, their joy was overwhelming, for they thought never to see the Princess alive again.

Suddenly, the palace came to life. In the stables, the horses neighed and shook their manes, the doves in the eaves began to coo once more, and even the dragonflies continued their flights. In the kitchen, the fire sprang up and the cook and his lazy boy awoke and stared a moment in surprise. Then the lad got the cuff on the ears he had deserved for one hundred years. The thick tangle of briars fell away and disappeared and in the surrounding countryside, tales of the reappearance of the castle filled the gossip of every house, night fire, and tavern for leagues around.

By and by the wedding was announced and the King spared no expense in inviting all. The marriage was celebrated grandly. So great was the love of Aurora and the Prince that their joy spread throughout the kingdom. By their many good and kindly deeds, they became revered by the people. To the end of their days, they lived happy and contented lives and thus the story of Briar Rose, who we now know as Sleeping Beauty, is remembered even till this day.